When Santa Sle

by
Deb Drinkall

For
Ellis and Gabriel

'*Twas* the night before Christmas and all advent doors,
Had been opened from 1 right up to 24.
Apart from one calendar next to the bed,
Of a white-bearded, snoring and loud sleepyhead.

He had been having a wonderful dream,
Of juicy mince pies topped with ketchup and cream!
His lips smacking loudly with a '*Nom Nom. Ho! Ho!*' as he
dreamt of his 100th mince pie in a row!

When into the room with a shriek and a shout,
Came an Elf screeching 'Santa! Wake up! Quick, get out!
Oh pickle! Oh trouble! Just look at the date!
Our calendar's wrong - we are going to be late!'

The snuggled up Santa slowly opened one eye,
as the Elf hopped around and gave a deep sigh.
'Oh giddies, ba-jinglies and jubbelly-poo!' said Santa,
'Whatever on earth will we do?!'

The little Elf flushed as he hopped in the air,
Santa glanced at the page with a look of despair.
The calendar's doors had indeed become jumbled,
'Bring me some coffee!' he was heard to have mumbled.

Ten minutes later and dressed all in red,
Santa had worked out a plan in his head.
'Okay now Elves, listen. Please all gather round' he began,
As he paced in his boots up and down.

'If we don't get these presents, if we don't get these toys,
Into the homes of these young girls and boys,
The magic of Christmas will forever be lost,
and that my dear Elves, is a very high cost!'

'So now we must find a delivery team,
The most magnificent there ever has been,'
'I'm thinking of characters, from books, my dear Elves.
Lets wake them all up, get them down from their shelves!'

'We need witches with broomsticks, to fly through the air.
We need clever princesses with very long hair.'
'We need bears, we need wizards and wolves dressed as sheep,
We need three little pigs... oh, and Little Bo Peep!'

'Wake them up, shake them up, free from their pages.
Hurry up now! For we haven't got ages!'

THE LION, THE WITCH, AND THE WARDROBE

Grimm's Fairy

Three Little Pigs

A Little Princess

Cinderella

LITTLE BO PEEP AND OTHER RHYMES

Rapunzel

Aesop's Fables

Goldilocks and the Three Bears

LITTLE RED RIDING HOOD

So the Elves sent the message and soon every book,
On every bookshelf, the pages they shook.
And the characters very quietly crept,
Away from the bookshelves, as the children still slept...

If you'd happened to gaze through your window that night,
The sights you had seen, would have brought great delight...
For every book hero you have read about,
Was part of a squad helping Santa Claus out.

The three bears had boxes, of 3 different sizes,
While Goldilocks' stockings were packed with surprises.
Fairies flew high - presents tied to their wings,
While hungry wolves carried the yummiest things.

Never before had they all worked together,
But they must! Or Christmas would be ruined forever!

When it came to getting the gifts down the chimney,
Santa had thought of a clever delivery.
A team of smart spiders had been given the task,
Of spinning silk nets that could hold strong and fast.

And into the chimneys the presents they'd dangle,
Slowly, with care, making sure not to tangle!
Then once every present was dropped on the floor,
The spiders had just to do one small job more...

Collect all the carrots, knock over the milk,
Grab the mince pies, tightly wound in their silk.
Then wind them back up without dropping a crumb,
The job was not finished 'til all this was done!

Some hours later and every last toy,
Had been safely delivered to each girl and boy.
And every character, from every book was tucked back inside
and away they'd been put.

And Santa returned to his home, to his bed,
Took off his shoes, scratched his weary, tired head.
Snuggled down deep and rested his eyes,
Thought once again about those yummy mince pies.

And as he drifted off, into his sleep so tight, sighed...

'Merry Christmas to all, and to all, a good night!'

The End

Printed in Great Britain
by Amazon